IN THE NIGHT

First U. S. Edition 1992

First published in Great Britain in 1991 by Collins Children's
Division, a division of HarperCollins Publishers.

ISBN 0-316-78586-5

Library of Congress Catalog Card Number 90-53692
Library of Congress Cataloging-in-Publication information
is available.

10 9 8 7 6 5 4 3 2 1

Printed in the People's Republic of China

This book is set in 24/30 Galliard.

IN THE NIGHT

☆ JONATHAN SHIPTON ☆

Illustrated by Gill Scriven

Little, Brown and Company
Boston Toronto London

This is me waking up
in the night.

This is everyone else fast asleep.

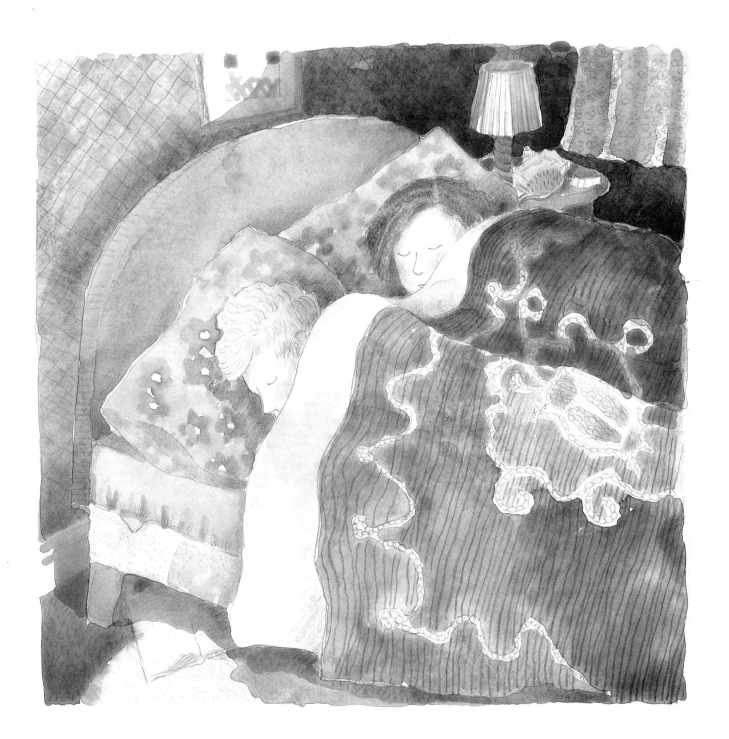

This is me creeping out of bed,

putting on my bathrobe,

tiptoeing to the window,

peeping through the curtains.

This is the dark
outside my window.

This is the tree
with the shivering leaves,
that grows in the dark,
outside my window.

This is the star that shines through the night.

This is the moon sparkling white.

This is the cat
with the glittering eyes,
that prowls through the shadows,
outside my window.

This is the cat,
that jumps on the branch,
that grows in the dark,
outside my window.

These are the clouds,
that chase through the sky,

and blacken the moon,
and the starlight.

This is the wind that rattles and sighs,
that shakes my window,
and shivers the leaves.

This is the cat with the
glittering eyes,
that springs off the branch,
that grows on the tree,
that lives in the dark,
outside my window.

And these are my freezing cold feet.

And that is my lovely warm bed.

And this is me jumping inside

and falling fast a . . . sleep . . .